REBEL POWER!

Written by Lauren Nesworthy

Editors Lauren Nesworthy, Anant Sagar
Art Editor Dimple Vohra
Assistant Art Editor Akansha Jain
Senior Art Editor Clive Savage
DTP Designer Umesh Singh Rawat
Pre-Production Producer Marc Staples
Pre-Production Manager Sunil Sharma
Producer David Appleyard
Managing Editors Sadie Smith,
Chitra Subramanyam
Managing Art Editors Neha Ahuja,
Ron Stobbart
Art Director Lisa Lanzarini
Publisher Julie Ferris
Publishing Director Simon Beecroft

Reading Consultant Maureen Fernandes

For Lucasfilm
Executive Editor Jonathan W. Rinzler
Art Director Troy Alders
Story Group Rayne Roberts, Pablo Hidalgo, Leland Chee

First published in Great Britain in 2015
by Dorling Kindersley Limited
80 Strand, London, WC2R 0RL
A Penguin Random House Company

10 9 8 7 6 5 4 3 2 1
001–279704–July/2015

Page design copyright © 2015 Dorling Kindersley Limited

© & TM 2015 LUCASFILM LTD.

All Rights Reserved. Used under Authorisation.

A CIP catalogue record for this book is available from the British Library.

ISBN: 978-0-24119-616-8

Printed in China

A WORLD OF IDEAS:
SEE ALL THERE IS TO KNOW

www.starwars.com
www.dk.com

Contents

Fighting for Lothal

Since the Empire took over the galaxy, things have been hard for the citizens of the planet Lothal.

But a brave group of rebels
is fighting back against the
Imperial army. This is bringing
hope to the people!

Ezra's Album

I look pretty good in uniform. →

Check out this graffiti in my room. Sabine made it just for me. ↗

Shh... My Master is meditating. ←

Hera the super pilot! She can outfly any TIE.

Haha! Zeb stinks so bad.

Chopper...?! You ruined my lunch.

Force Training

The Jedi Kanan believes
that the Force is strong
with young Ezra.
In-between missions,
Kanan teaches Ezra
how to use his powers.
He shows him what it
truly means to be a Jedi.

HOW TO BECOME A JEDI

Focus is important to master the Force.

Learn new skills like the Force pull, Force jump and Force push.

The Force enables you to communicate with many kinds of animals.

Prove you are worthy by going through the tough trials. The trials are a test of skill, strength and wisdom.

Pass the tests to obtain a special crystal and make your own lightsaber.

You are now on your way to becoming a Jedi Knight.

Rebel Attack

The rebels are always
finding ways to ruin things
for the Empire.

The celebrations on Empire Day grind to a halt when Sabine's amazing explosions destroy a brand new TIE fighter!

REBEL SKILLS

The rebels are armed with a variety of skills. They use these abilities as they fight the Empire.

Sabine is a weapons expert. Her speciality is making explosives.

SABINE

Hera pilots the *Ghost*. She can outfly the best Imperial pilots.

HERA

Ezra is a Padawan. He is training to become a Jedi Knight.

EZRA

Zeb is a strong warrior. He loves to fight against stormtroopers.

ZEB

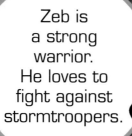

Kanan is a Jedi. He leads the rebels in their fight against the Empire.

KANAN

Chopper is a great mechanic. He keeps the *Ghost* in superb shape.

CHOPPER

Imperial Influence

The Imperials try to
make people believe
that being ruled by the
Empire is a good thing.
They do this by
using posters and
Holonews messages.
This helps the Empire
keep everyone under
their control.

BE A
GOOD
CITIZEN

**PEOPLE OF LOTHAL!
YOU ARE ALL
PROUD MEMBERS
OF THE EMPIRE.**

**Remember that
the Empire will only do
what is good for you.**

HERE IS HOW YOU CAN HELP

Obey the Empire's instructions.

Help us track down traitors.

Report all criminals to the nearest Imperial officer.

Support the Empire and its soldiers.

Always celebrate Empire Day.

- By order of Agent Kallus

Ezra Undercover

Fighting isn't always the best
way to stop the Empire.
Sometimes the rebels have
to be sneaky.
Ezra pretends to be a stormtrooper
cadet at the Imperial Academy.
This gives him a chance to
steal important plans that can
help the rebels.

New Allies

Sometimes new friends can
come from unexpected places.
Ezra meets two stormtrooper
cadets, Zare Leonis and Jai
Kell, who help him with his
mission at the Academy.
The rebels are making
more allies!

BECOME A STORMTROOPER

Join the Imperial Academy:
Serve the Empire with pride!

Be part of a team.

Fight against the rebels.

Learn military tactics.

Use deadly weapons.

ALSO, GET AN
AWESOME SUIT
OF ARMOUR!

Stealing Secrets

The Empire may be scary, but that does not stop people from standing up to them.

The rebels rescue a Rodian named Tseebo from the Imperials. He knows many secrets about the Empire, which he shares with the rebels.

Fight the Empire

The rebels know that it's not easy to beat the Empire, but that doesn't stop them from trying. They are always thinking of new ways to succeed.

☑ Help the people of Lothal.

●→ ☑ Collect weapons, food and equipment.

●→ ☑ Blow up Imperial property.

●→ ☑ Master the use of the Force.

☑ Rescue prisoners from the Empire.

☑ Hack into the communication tower.

●→ ☑ Steal Imperial secrets.

☑ Do not get caught by the Empire.

Galactic Businessman

Smuggler Lando Calrissian does not always do the right thing. He has many skills, however, that can help the rebels. A smuggler makes a strong ally against the Empire!

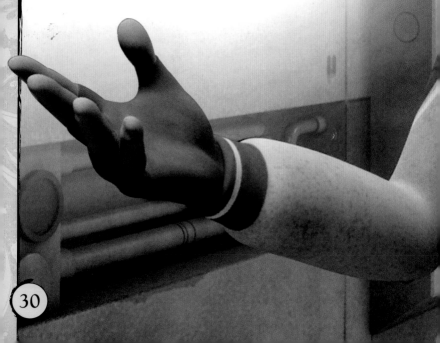

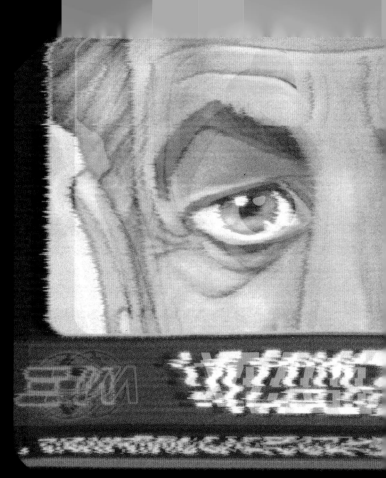

Double Agent

It is hard for the rebels to
know who to trust.

They thought that a man named
Gall Trayvis hated the Empire.

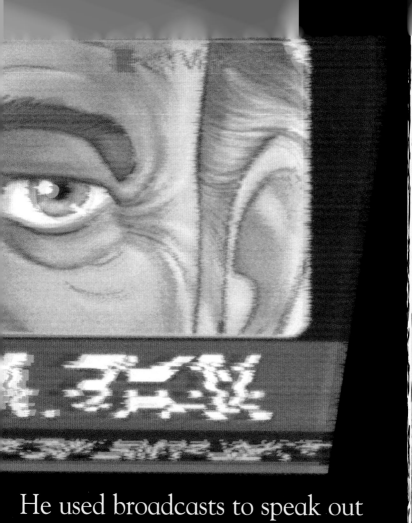

He used broadcasts to speak out
against the Empire and gave the
rebels information using codes.
But he was secretly working for
the Empire all along!

A MESSAGE OF HOPE

The Empire is spreading lies about the rebels. So the rebels are sending out a message to the people of Lothal encouraging them to fight for their freedom.

We are rebels, fighting for the people... fighting for you.

...See what the Empire has done to your lives, your families and your freedom?

It's only gonna get worse... Unless we stand up and fight back...

Stand up, together. Because that's when we're strongest. As one.

Capturing Rebels

No matter how hard the Imperials try to stop the rebels, they are disappointed over and over again! Imperial Governor Grand Moff Tarkin will punish anyone who fails to defeat the rebels.

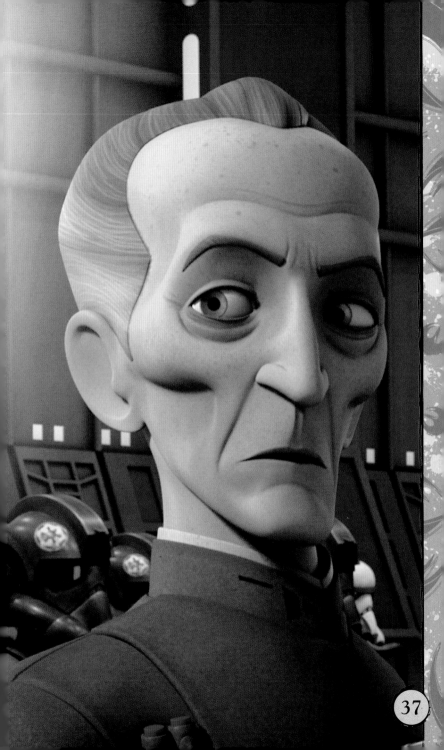

The Dark Lord

The rebels are growing
stronger every day!
The Imperials are afraid
that more people will
join them in the fight
against the Empire.
Only one man is
powerful enough to
stop the rebels once
and for all… Darth Vader.

Quiz

1. Who is teaching Ezra how to use his powers?

2. What do you get if you pass the Jedi Trials?

3. What does Sabine's explosion destroy on Empire Day?

4. Who is a great mechanic?

5. Who were Ezra's friends at the Imperial Academy?

6. Who is the Rodian that the rebels rescue from the Empire?

7. What is Lando's job?

8. Who is a double agent?

9. Who is the Imperial Governor?

10. Who is powerful enough to stop the rebels?

Answers on page 45

Glossary

Meditating
Thinking calmly.

Undercover
Working in a secret way to collect information.

Tactics
A plan for achieving a goal.

Smuggler
Someone who transports things secretly.

Double agent
Someone who pretends to work for one
person, when they are actually working
for someone else.

Speciality
Something that a person is particularly good at.

Distraction
Something that makes it hard to pay attention.

Padawan
Someone who is training to become a Jedi.

Index

Answers to the quiz on pages 42 and 43:
1. Kanan 2. A special crystal 3. TIE fighter 4. Chopper
5. Zare Leonis and Jai Kell 6. Tseebo 7. Smuggler
8. Gall Trayvis 9. Grand Moff Tarkin 10. Darth Vader

Guide for Parents

DK Reads is a three-level reading series for children, developing the habit of reading widely for both pleasure and information. These books have exciting running text interspersed with a range of reading genres to suit your child's reading ability, as required by the school curriculum. Each book is designed to develop your child's reading skills, fluency, grammar awareness and comprehension in order to build confidence and engagement when reading.

Ready for a *Beginning to Read* book
YOUR CHILD SHOULD

- be using phonics, including combinations of consonants, such as bl, gl and sm, to read unfamiliar words; and common word endings, such as plurals, ing, ed and ly.

- be using the storyline, illustrations and the grammar of a sentence to check and correct their own reading.

- be pausing briefly at commas, and for longer at full stops; and altering his/her expression to respond to question, exclamation and speech marks.

A Valuable and Shared Reading Experience

For many children, reading requires much effort but adult participation can make this both fun and easier. So here are a few tips on how to use this book with your child.

TIP 1 Check out the contents together before your child begins:

- Read the text about the book on the back cover.
- Read through and discuss the contents page together to heighten your child's interest and expectation.
- Briefly discuss any unfamiliar or difficult words on the contents page.

- Chat about the non-fiction reading features used in the book, such as headings, captions, recipes, lists or charts.

This introduction helps to put your child in control and makes the reading challenge less daunting.

TIP 2 Support your child as he/she reads the story pages:

- Give the book to your child to read and turn the pages.

- Where necessary, encourage your child to break a word into syllables, sound out each one and then flow the syllables together. Ask him/her to reread the sentence to check the meaning.

- When there's a question mark or an exclamation mark, encourage your child to vary his/her voice as he/she reads the sentence. Demonstrate how to do this if it is helpful.

TIP 3 Praise, share and chat:

- The factual pages tend to be more difficult than the story pages, and are designed to be shared with your child.

- Ask questions about the text and the meaning of the words used. Ask your child to suggest his/her own quiz questions. These help to develop comprehension skills and awareness of the language used.

A FEW ADDITIONAL TIPS

- Try and read together everyday. Little and often is best. These books are divided into manageable chapters for one reading session. However after 10 minutes, only keep going if your child wants to read on.

- Always encourage your child to have a go at reading difficult words by themselves. Praise any self-corrections, for example, "I like the way you sounded out that word and then changed the way you said it, to make sense".

- Read other books of different types to your child just for enjoyment and information.

Have you read these other great books from DK?

BEGINNING TO READ

Meet a band of rebels, brave enough to take on the Empire!

The Inquisitor is coming. Now there is no safe place for the Jedi to hide!

Roar! Thud! Meet the dinosaurs. Who do you think is the deadliest?

STARTING TO READ ALONE

Join David on an amazing trip to meet elephants in Asia and Africa.

Follow Chris Croc's adventures from a baby to a mighty king.

Join the heroes of the rebellion as they continue to fight the Empire.